I'm the Biggest Thing in the OCEAN

by Kevin Sherry

Dial Books for Young Readers

I'm a GIANT squid
and I'm BIG.

I'm bigger than these shrimp.

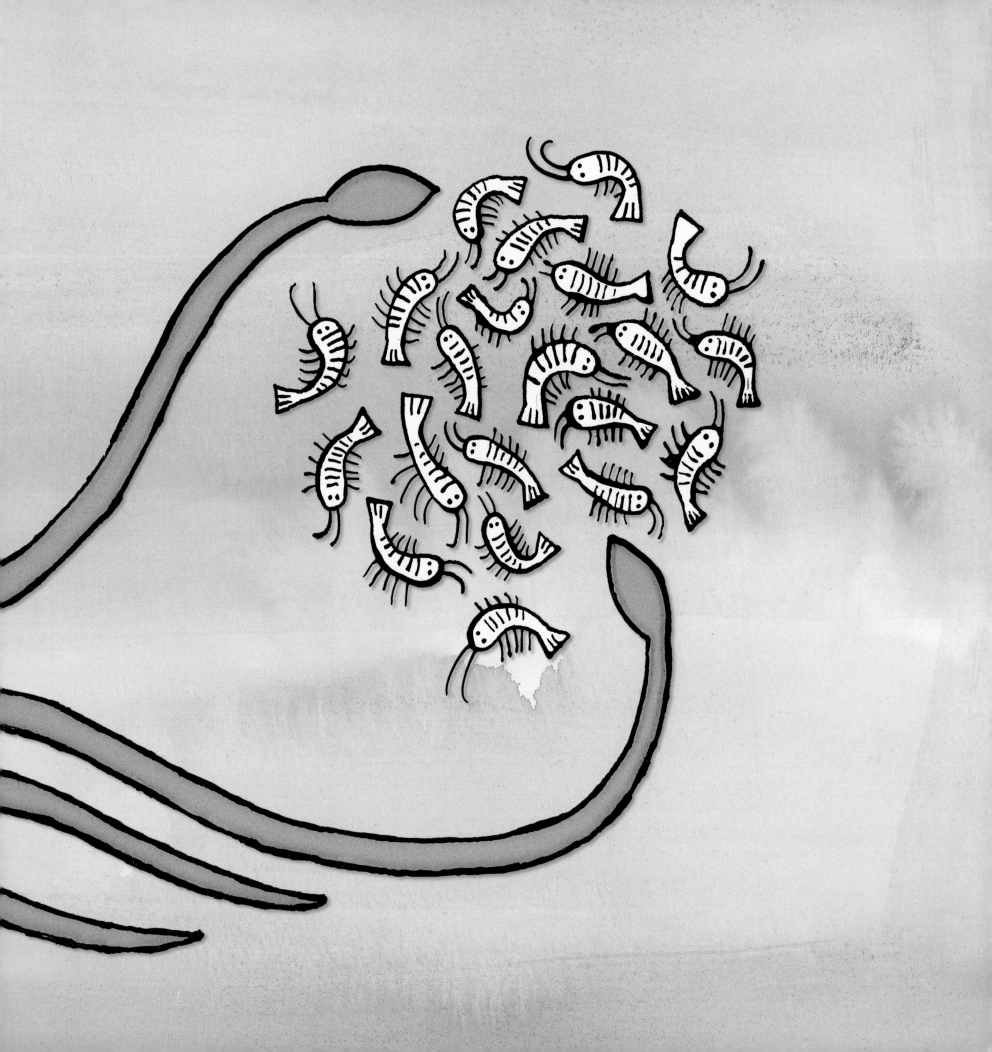

I'm
bigger
than
these
clams.

I'm bigger
than
this
crab.

I'm bigger than that jellyfish.

I'm bigger than these turtles.

I'm even
bigger than
this
octopus.

this fish.

and that fish.

that fish,

this fish,

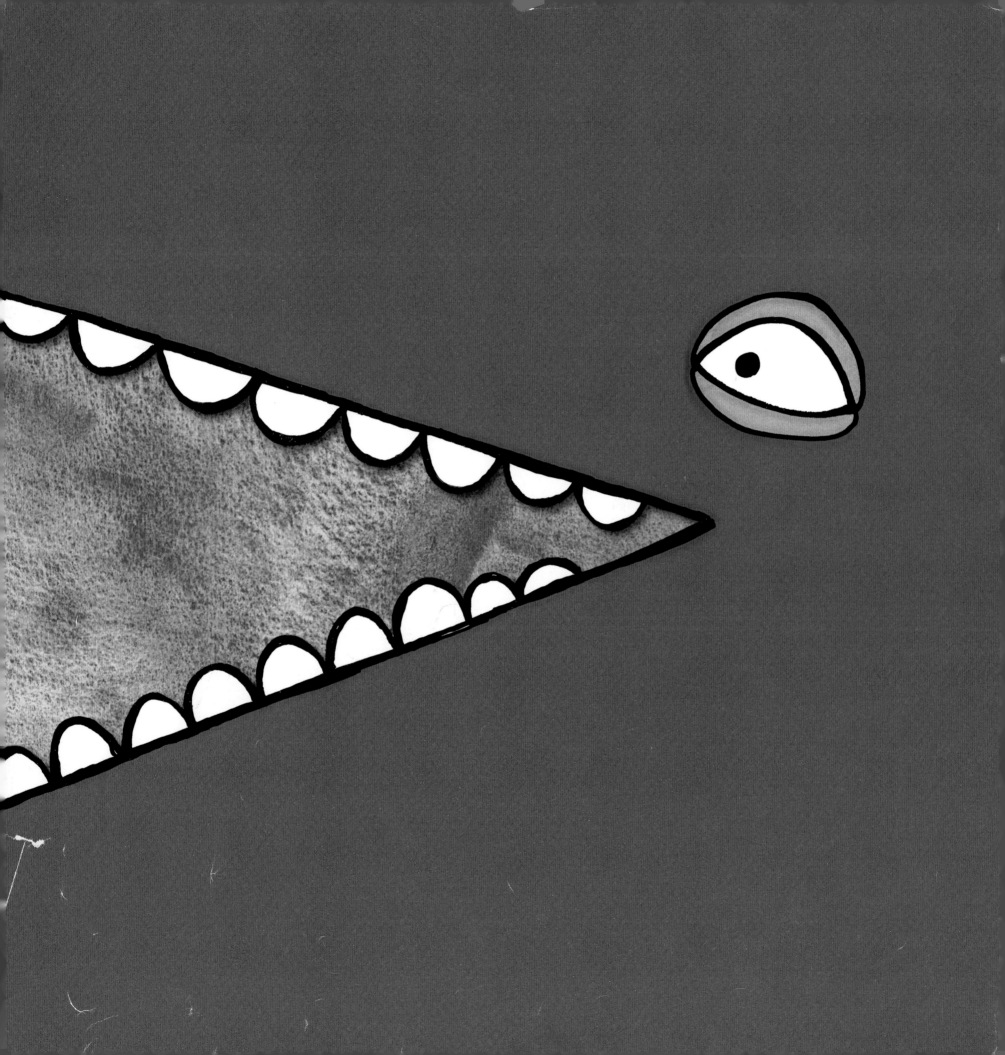

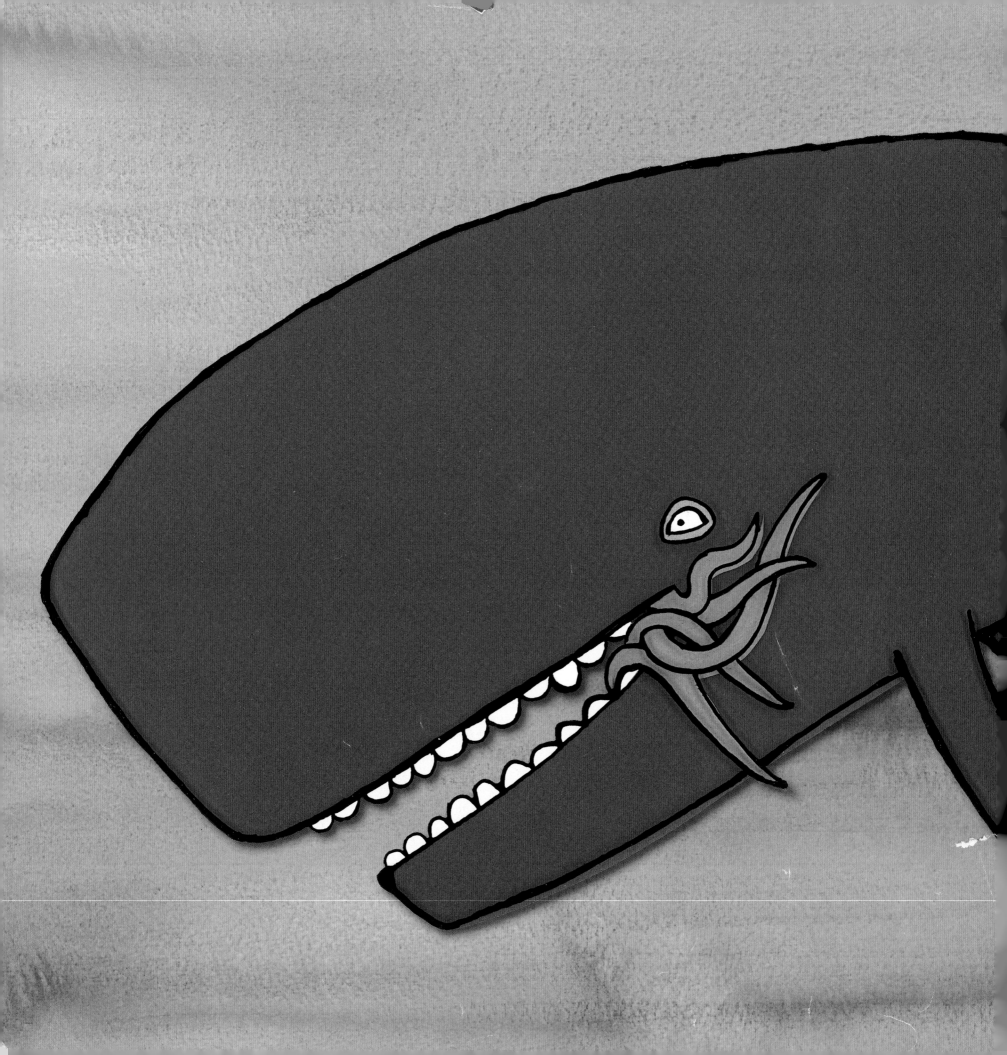

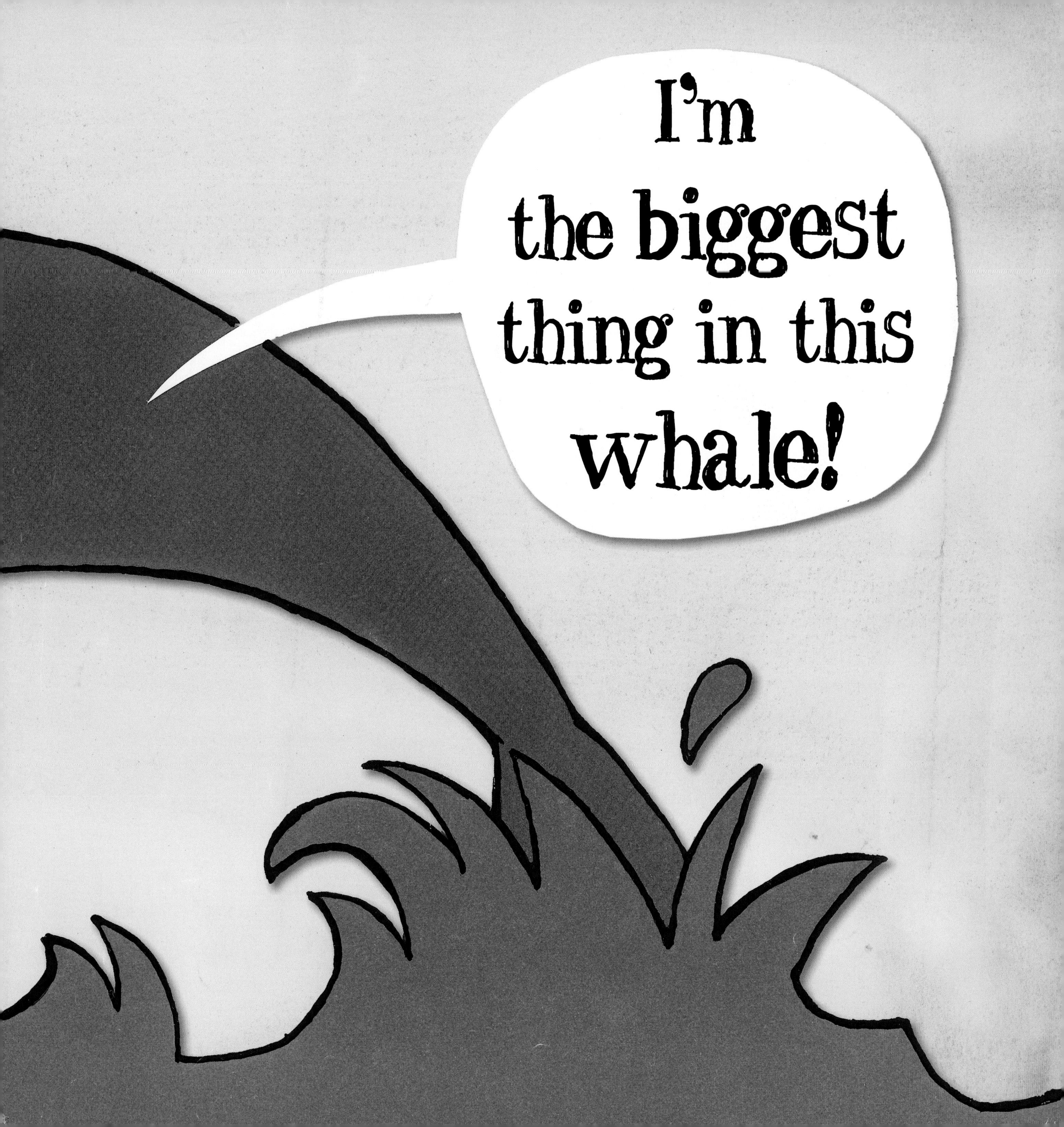
I'm the biggest thing in this whale!

I'm bigger than plankton

To my parents, who were always the biggest thing in my ocean

DIAL BOOKS FOR YOUNG READERS • A division of Penguin Young Readers Group • Published by The Penguin Group •
Penguin Group (USA) Inc., 375 Hudson Street, New York, NY 10014, U.S.A. • Penguin Group (Canada), 90 Eglinton Avenue
East, Suite 700, Toronto, Ontario, Canada M4P 2Y3 (a division of Pearson Penguin Canada Inc.) • Penguin Books Ltd, 80
Strand, London WC2R 0RL, England. • Penguin Ireland, 25 St. Stephen's Green, Dublin 2, Ireland (a division of Penguin
Books Ltd.) • Penguin Books India Pvt Ltd, 11 Community Centre, Panchsheel Park, New Delhi - 110 017, India. • Penguin
Group (NZ), Cnr Airborne and Rosedale Roads, Albany, Auckland, New Zealand (a division of Pearson New Zealand Ltd). •
Penguin Books (South Africa) (Pty) Ltd, 24 Sturdee Avenue, Rosebank, Johannesburg 2196, South Africa. • Penguin Books
Ltd, Registered Offices: 80 Strand, London WC2R 0RL, England.

The publisher does not have any control over and does not assume any responsibility for author
or third-party websites or their content.
Designed by Teresa Kietlinski Dikun
Text set in Bookman, Blue Century
Manufactured in China on acid-free paper

20 19 18 17 16 15 14 13

Library of Congress Cataloging-in-Publication Data
Sherry, Kevin.
I'm the biggest thing in the ocean / by Kevin Sherry.
    p. cm.
Summary: A giant squid brags about being bigger than everything else in the ocean—almost.
ISBN-13: 978-0-8037-3192-9
[1. Giant squids—Fiction. 2. Squids—Fiction. 3. Marine animals—Fiction. 4. Size—Fiction.] I. Title.
PZ7.S549Im 2007
[E]—dc22
2006027815

The art was completed in three layers, each separated by glass that was pried from the windows of shipwrecked pirate ships.
There is a watercolor layer background, then a cut-paper level, and finally, an ink layer consisting of 100% fresh squid ink.